MOUSE SCOUTS

Camp Out

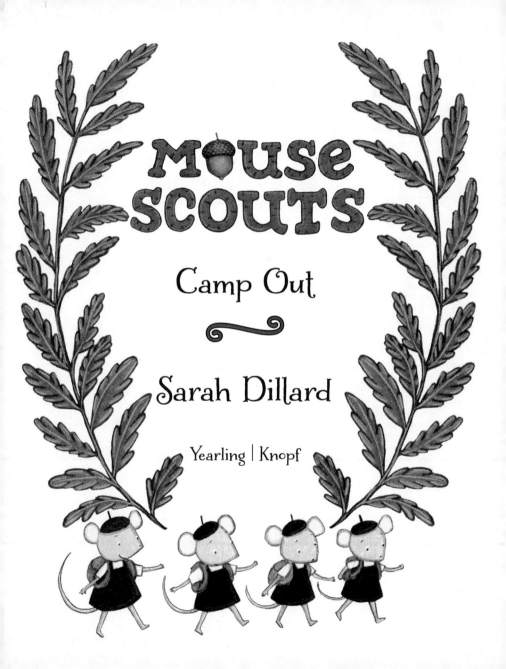

MOUSE SCOUTS

Camp Out

Sarah Dillard

Yearling | Knopf

This is a work of fiction. Names, characters, places, and incidents either are the product of the author's imagination or are used fictitiously. Any resemblance to actual persons, living or dead, events, or locales is entirely coincidental.

Copyright © 2016 by Sarah Dillard

All rights reserved. Published in the United States by Alfred A. Knopf, an imprint of Random House Children's Books, a division of Penguin Random House LLC, New York.

Knopf, Borzoi Books, and the colophon are registered trademarks of Penguin Random House LLC.

Visit us on the Web! randomhousekids.com

Educators and librarians, for a variety of teaching tools, visit us at RHTeachersLibrarians.com

Library of Congress Cataloging-in-Publication Data
Names: Dillard, Sarah, author.
Title: Camp out / Sarah Dillard.
Description: First edition. I New York : Alfred A. Knopf, [2016] I
Series: Mouse Scouts ; 3 I
Summary: "The Mouse Scouts are hitting the nature trail to earn their 'Camp Out' badge. But not all of the troopers are gung-ho about sleeping beneath the stars. When Miss Poppy goes missing, can the Scouts work together to track down their troop leader?" —Provided by publisher
Identifiers: LCCN 2016001273 (print) I LCCN 2016026345 (ebook) I
ISBN 978-0-385-75609-9 (lib. bdg.) I ISBN 978-0-385-75608-2 (pbk.) I
ISBN 978-0-385-75610-5 (ebook)
Subjects: I CYAC: Scouting (Youth activity)—Fiction. I Camping—Fiction. I
Mice—Fiction. I BISAC: JUVENILE FICTION / Animals / General. I JUVENILE
FICTION / Nature & the Natural World / General (see also headings under Animals). I JUVENILE FICTION / Family / General
(see also headings under Social Issues).
Classification: LCC PZ7.D57733 Cam 2016 (print) I
LCC PZ7.D57733 (ebook) I DDC [Fic]—dc23

Printed in the United States of America
October 2016
10 9 8 7 6 5 4 3 2 1

First Edition

For Fiske, the best neighbor!

Contents

CHAPTER 1

~ ❦ ~

Preparing for Adventure

Up until now, becoming a
Mouse Scout was the best
thing that had ever happened
to Violet. But all that changed
when Miss Poppy announced
that the Acorn Scouts would
be going on an overnight
camping trip to earn their
"Camp Out" badge.

Violet could still hear Miss Poppy's shrill voice in her head as she started arranging her camping supplies. "We are going to hike through the wilderness until we find

a suitable spot for setting up camp," Miss Poppy had said. "Then we will forage for healthy nuts and delicious berries to prepare a filling, nutritious meal. After the sun goes down, we'll have a campfire and sing songs. Trips like this are what Mouse Scout memories are made of!"

But Violet wasn't fooled by any of that. She was pretty sure camping was going to be horrible. Nature was *okay*, and she liked gardens and playing in the park. But the wilderness was a whole different story. It was a scary place, full of danger. She'd be lucky to get out of there alive.

Violet looked at all the things laid out on her bed. Then she checked her *Mouse Scout Handbook* to be sure she hadn't forgotten anything.

Acorn mess kit: check.

First-aid kit: check.

Toothbrush: check.

Change of clothing: check.

2 rubber bands: check.

Emergency whistle: check.

Orange safety blanket: check.

Just in case the foraging didn't work out, Violet added an emergency pack of six sunflower seeds and two raisins. She wanted to be prepared.

One by one, she placed all the items in her regulation backpack. The last thing to go in was her orange safety blanket, and as she pushed it down to make it fit, she heard something crack. *I hope that wasn't my acorn mess kit,* she thought.

Now that her bed was cleared, Violet could finally go to sleep. Violet *loved* her bed. Her pillow was stuffed with soft cotton balls, and her mattress was a quilted eyeglass pouch filled with downy feathers.

Tomorrow night she would be sleeping on the cold, hard ground. Violet shivered at the thought.

A few houses away, Tigerlily could hardly wait for the camping trip. When she joined the Mouse Scouts, she had high hopes for adventure. But it seemed like all they ever did was make boring crafts or try to make the world a better place. That might satisfy Violet, but

Tigerlily wanted to do something exciting. And the day had finally come! They were going to earn their "Camp Out" badge. It didn't get much better than that.

Tigerlily didn't need to look at the
Mouse Scout Handbook. She had her
own ideas about what to pack. She had
already pulled a few essential supplies
from her emergency wagon that she
thought would be useful. She threw a
toothpick, a small roll of duct tape, and a

zipper pull into her backpack. Then she fixed a paper clip and a rubber band to the outside. She picked up a twist tie and studied it. "You never know what will come in handy," she said as she stuffed it in her backpack.

When she was done, Tigerlily looked at her rumpled bed. It still had a few things on it that were never going to fit in her backpack.

She decided to sleep on the floor instead. "It's almost like sleeping on the ground," she said. "I might as well start camping now!"

MOUSE SCOUT HANDBOOK

Packing Your Backpack

A well-packed backpack is the key to an enjoyable and memorable camping trip. Imagine the horror of stopping to set up camp only to find that you have forgotten your acorn mess kit or that your emergency whistle is broken.

A few days before your trip, make a checklist of the things you will need. When you have gathered all your items, lay them out in one place. Organize the items in the order that you will place them in your pack. Larger and heavier items should go in the bottom, while lighter items and things that could get crushed should be near the top. *What* you pack and *how* you pack can make or break your camping trip.

A well-packed backpack includes:

- ☑ An acorn mess kit
- ☑ A change of clothes
- ☑ An orange safety blanket
- ☑ An emergency whistle
- ☑ A snack, and some water
- ☐ A first-aid kit

An acorn mess kit

Cap can be used as a small bowl or cup.

Bottom can be used as a large bowl for cooking or eating.

Utensils can be stored inside.

A change of clothes

An orange
safety blanket
(for warmth
and visibility)

An emergency whistle

A snack, and some water
to be saved in case of
emergency

FIRST-AID KIT

A first-aid kit, including
cotton swab tips, and
antiseptic

Tiny jewel or pillbox

Rolls of cloth or
strips of paper towels

Cotton swab tips
(sawed in half for
easier packing)

CHAPTER 2

Welcome to the Wilderness

The next morning, Violet left her soft warm bed and dressed in her Mouse Scout uniform. But when she put on her backpack, she nearly crumbled under the weight. "I'll never make it!" Violet moaned as she slowly started walking to the park.

"Hey, Violet, wait up!" Tigerlily came trotting up behind her. Violet groaned.

"This is going to be the best badge

EVER!" Tigerlily gushed as she ran in a little circle around Violet. Violet smiled weakly. Tigerlily was her best friend, but sometimes her enthusiasm for all things adventurous could be annoying.

"Not even Miss Poppy can ruin the fun this time," Tigerlily said.

Tigerlily jogged ahead while Violet trudged along behind her. When they reached the meeting spot at the edge of the park, the other Scouts were already there.

Cricket's pack was bulging at the seams. She could barely stand under the weight.

"What in the world do you have in there?" Tigerlily asked.

"Cheese, mostly," Cricket declared. "This is all about survival, isn't it? I couldn't survive without cheese."

"Good point," said Tigerlily. "But cheese isn't going to protect you from wild animals."

Violet gulped. Wild animals? Miss Poppy hadn't said anything about wild animals.

Petunia tugged at one of the rubber bands hanging from Tigerlily's pack. "I'm not sure any of this junk will protect you either."

"You'd be surprised," said Tigerlily.

"You don't *really* think there will be wild animals out there, do you?" Violet was getting more and more nervous.

"I'm more concerned about tick-borne diseases and leaf mold," Junebug said. Her voice was muffled by her neck scarf, which she had pulled up over her nose to protect herself from allergens. Junebug had a sensitive system.

Tigerlily noticed something satiny poking out of Hyacinth's backpack. "What's that?" she asked.

"The *Mouse Scout Handbook* said we had to make our own beds," said Hyacinth, "so I brought my favorite sheets from home. I hope they fit the beds at the camp. I can *only* sleep on satin sheets."

"Are there going to be beds?" asked Violet hopefully.

Tigerlily just laughed. "Don't you two know *anything* about camping?" she asked. "It's all about being in nature. We'll be making our own beds out of leaves and moss. That's what the handbook meant!"

Hyacinth gaped at Tigerlily. "You

 mean I have to sleep on the *ground*? On *moss*? What about bugs? What about dirt? I can't possibly sleep in those conditions!"

"Just wait until you hear about the bathroom!" Petunia giggled.

A sharp tweet from a Mouse Scout emergency whistle announced Miss Poppy's arrival. Only Mouse Scout leaders were allowed to use their whistle in non-emergency situations.

The Scouts stood at attention.

"All right, Scouts! Here are a few things to keep in mind before we start," said Miss Poppy. "We are entering a WILDERNESS

AREA. The wilderness may look beautiful, but it is full of HIDDEN DANGER. Keep track of your surroundings. Stay together and stay on the trail. DO NOT go off by yourself. If you find yourself separated from the group, STAY WHERE YOU ARE until help arrives. Beware of biting insects, and animals and birds that prey on small animals—including mice. Do not speak to animals that you do not know. Do NOT put anything in your mouth that you find in the woods until it has been identified by ME as edible. And whatever you do, never, ever touch POISON IVY."

Violet shuddered. Poison ivy? She took a deep breath and raised her hand. "Miss Poppy, what is poison ivy?"

"Poison ivy is a noxious weed. It runs rampant through the woods. Touching poison ivy can cause a terrible itchy rash with blisters. And it looks like THAT!" Miss Poppy shouted, and pointed toward the entrance of the Left Meadow Nature Trail.

Violet looked, but she had no idea which plant Miss Poppy meant. They all looked the same to her.

Violet shut her eyes tight and held her tail. "I wish it was already tomorrow and we were done. I don't know how I will ever survive."

MOUSE SCOUT HANDBOOK

It's Wild Out There!

What could be more wonderful than spending time in the great outdoors! As beautiful as nature is, never forget that it can be dangerous, too. Always be aware of your surroundings and keep an eye out for potential hazards. Being prepared can make your wilderness experience enjoyable and enriching.

WILDERNESS DANGERS

Poisonous plants: Poison ivy, poison oak, poison sumac. Contact with these plants can cause terrible rashes.

Poison Ivy

Poison Oak

Poison Sumac

All mushrooms: Many are poisonous. To be safe, do not touch, climb, or sit on them.

Biting and stinging insects: Ticks, mosquitoes, wasps, and hornets. Insects can carry disease, and their bites can be painful.

Predators: Foxes, snakes, and owls are known to hunt mice. Avoid these fiends at all costs!

Other wild animals will be more interested in any food that you are carrying. Be sure to secure your food safely, and do not store food in your tent, especially when you are sleeping!

CHAPTER 3

The Hike

Miss Poppy led the Scouts to the entrance of the Left Meadow Nature Trail, and the hike began. Before long, the Scouts were surrounded by ferns. Tall trees blocked the sunlight. Violet squinted to adjust to the darkness.

"Take a deep breath, Scouts," said Miss Poppy. "That is pure, fresh, wilderness air. Doesn't it make you feel alive?"

Violet gulped as much air as she could. It seemed just like the same old air she always breathed. She didn't feel any more alive than she usually did; in fact, it didn't even feel much like wilderness. She could still hear the sprinkler system in the park behind them. She also noticed that the menacing squirrel from the park was darting through the trees ahead. Her shoulders ached from her backpack, and they were just getting started!

Meanwhile, Tigerlily darted back and forth across the trail, climbing up trees and leaping from branch to branch overhead just as the squirrel was doing.

"Stay on the ground, Tigerlily!" Miss Poppy said. "And stay away from the wildlife. Remember, squirrels can't be trusted."

Tigerlily hopped to the ground and trudged alongside Violet.

The squirrel giggled and threw a nut at Tigerlily. It hit the ground right in front of her.

"Hey!" Tigerlily shouted, but the squirrel just laughed and threw another nut.

"Do not provoke him, Tigerlily," Miss Poppy scolded.

Tigerlily fell back in line with Violet. "He started it," she muttered.

Violet shrugged and smiled at Tigerlily, but she wasn't having any fun either. She tried to keep up with Tigerlily but soon found herself lagging behind.

Before long, Hyacinth and Petunia had passed her, too. They were arguing about the comforts of camping. "I still can't believe we won't have beds!" Hyacinth cried. "You're probably going to tell me they don't have fluffy towels in the bathroom either."

That's Camping!

"That's camping," said Petunia.

Tigerlily darted ahead of the troop and circled back. She stuck her tongue out at the squirrel when Miss Poppy wasn't looking. When she got back to Violet, she had a hard time going at Violet's pace.

"Maybe it would be easier if you tried walking a little faster," Tigerlily said.

Violet glared at her as she huffed and puffed.

"Keep the chitchat to a minimum, Scouts," Miss Poppy said. "Let's appreciate nature's music."

Violet was too out of breath to appreciate anything.

As if on cue, the squirrel that had been following them cackled so loudly that Violet jumped, and her hat fell off. As she bent down to pick it up, Junebug and Cricket ambled ahead of her. Junebug was sniffling from allergies while Cricket nibbled a Cheese Crispit she had taken from her backpack.

"I hope you are not leaving crumbs, Cricket," Miss Poppy said. "Any kind of litter will disturb nature's fine balance."

Tigerlily pointed to a line of ants marching away, holding Cheese Crispit crumbs high above their heads. "They seem to be balancing just fine," she said, and giggled.

"If I have to ask you to be quiet one more time, it will be straight back to Buttercups for everyone," Miss Poppy said.

"This would be so much more fun without Miss Poppy," Tigerlily whispered to Violet.

"I suppose it could be worse," said Violet. "At least it's not raining."

Just then, there was a loud clap of thunder.

MOUSE SCOUT HANDBOOK

Take a Hike!

Hiking is a wonderful way to explore nature and get exercise at the same time. All you need is comfortable clothing and the great outdoors.

When you are hiking in the wilderness, stay on marked trails. Venturing off the trail cannot only get you lost but can also get you into serious trouble. You could fall off a cliff, slip on a wet rock, or be carried away in a fast-moving stream. Stay on the trail, and always hike with at least one other mouse.

Here are a few other tips to help you get the most out of the great outdoors safely:

- Before your hike, study a map of the area you will be exploring.

- Keep an eye on the weather, and be prepared for sudden changes in the conditions.

- Let someone know where you are going and when you expect to return.

- Always bring water and a snack.

- Do not litter or disturb the environment.

- Never go into the wilderness alone!

CHAPTER 4

Thunder!

"Uh-oh!" Violet gasped.

"I hate thunder!" Junebug shuddered. "My ears are very sensitive to loud noises."

"I don't mind thunder, but lightning is scary!" said Cricket.

"I LOVE thunder-storms!" Tigerlily said,

throwing her head back and waving her arms in the air.

"Thunderstorms are SERIOUS BUSI-NESS, Scouts," Miss Poppy said. "It is important to follow the proper thunderstorm procedure. Now listen up. Gather any plant material handy to provide cover.

Then, backpacks OFF, and squat DOWN. We want to stay as low to the ground as possible. Stay APART. Do not hold hands. Lightning can travel from one mouse to another."

Violet froze for a moment, imagining all the Mouse Scouts being struck by lightning. Then she joined the other Scouts in gathering leaves, ferns, and grass. Violet looked at her bundle of plants. Was any of it poison ivy? She still had no idea what it looked like!

There was a flash of lightning, and soon after, a loud crack of thunder sounded and the ground shook. Then it started to rain.

"We're going to drown!" Violet cried.

"My eyelashes are losing their curl!" complained Hyacinth.

"I wish my *tail* would," Petunia cracked.

"My cheese is getting soggy!" Cricket wailed.

"THIS IS CHARACTER BUILDING!" Miss Poppy shouted. The Scouts could hardly hear her over the sound of the storm.

"I don't need any more character," Tigerlily muttered.

Violet looked around. Everyone was wet and bedraggled. Junebug was shivering. Even Tigerlily was sulking. Camping

out was definitely the worst Mouse Scout activity ever.

As suddenly as the storm started, it stopped. Slowly the Scouts uncovered themselves and stood up. Once again it was a beautiful sunny day. The only difference was that they were surrounded by puddles and little streams.

"Pick up your backpacks," Miss Poppy said, "and let's head for drier land."

The Scouts began to wade across the stream. When they were nearly on the other side, Hyacinth slipped and fell. Junebug and Violet went to help her, but they slipped, too, and—*splash!*—in they both went! Finally the three girls managed to get up and make their way to dry land.

"I'm *drenched!*" Hyacinth cried. "And my uniform is completely *ruined!*"

"I'm catching a chill." Junebug sniffed.

She reached in her backpack and pulled out her orange safety blanket and wrapped it around herself.

Violet was miserable! She had had it with camping. She had had it with character building. She didn't even know if

she wanted to be a Mouse Scout anymore. This was *not* the stuff of Mouse Scout memories—it was more the stuff of Mouse Scout nightmares!

MOUSE SCOUT HANDBOOK

~~~~~~~~~~~~~~~~~~~~~~~~~~~~~~~~

Weathering the Storm

Weather conditions can change unexpectedly, especially in the wilderness. Be sure to pay attention to forecasts before heading out. If there is a chance of a storm, it might be a good idea to do something else for the day.

If you do find yourself caught in bad weather, don't panic. At the first sign of lightning or thunder, seek cover. Do not take shelter in trees or any other plant or structure that is in

danger of being struck by lightning. Woodchuck or chipmunk holes are good choices, as long as they are not in low-lying areas or near streambeds, which could flood.

If there is no shelter to be found, crouch down, making yourself as small as possible, while minimizing contact with the ground. Avoid open fields, low-lying areas, mountaintops, rocks, ponds, streams, and wetlands. Keep away from tall single trees.

Once the storm starts, stay where you are until it has passed. Luckily, thunderstorms tend to be fast moving, but beware—they often recur.

CHAPTER 5

Setting Up Camp

The Scouts trudged along behind Miss Poppy. Violet's wet uniform was cold and uncomfortable, but the sun was shining and, before long, it was almost dry. Suddenly Miss Poppy came to a stop.

"This is it!" Miss Poppy declared. "This is our campsite."

"This?" Hyacinth cried. "But there's nothing here!"

"That's nature for you!" Petunia said with a snicker.

There's nothing here!

Violet looked around. Hyacinth was right. They were standing in a small clearing. The ground was covered with pine needles, small pinecones, and a few roots. The trees around the clearing were tall, and the sunlight filtered down through their branches. It felt like true wilderness.

"Now, let's get to work, Scouts!" said Miss Poppy. "If you all read your *Mouse Scout Handbook* as instructed, you will know how to construct a simple shelter using twigs and leaves. Time is wasting. We have to get our campsite ready *and* forage for dinner before dark."

The Scouts got to work. First they swept the ground with pine needle brooms. Then they found moss for their beds. It was still damp from the storm, so they set it out in the sun.

While the moss was drying they gathered twigs, leaves, and more pine needles to make their tents.

They built frames with the twigs, then created walls and roofs using leaves, moss, and pinecones. By the time their tents were ready, the moss was dry and they could make their beds.

Even Hyacinth had to admit that the moss was surprisingly comfortable . . . although she still covered hers with her satin sheet.

Tigerlily sat and leaned back on the pinecone that she had set outside her tent.

"Just like home," she sighed. "Only better."

Violet turned to her own tent. The twigs were bending under the weight of the pinecone roof. One stiff breeze would probably knock the whole thing down. *No, she thought, home is much better than this!*

Hyacinth surveyed the campsite. Then she turned to Petunia. "So, about those bathrooms?" she asked.

Petunia pointed to the woods.

"I was afraid of that," Hyacinth said as she sauntered out of the clearing.

"Watch out for poison ivy!" Petunia called after her.

When the Scouts were done with their tents, Miss Poppy gave a sharp tweet of her whistle. "No time to rest on your laurels, Scouts. It's time to find our supper. Nothing tastes better than a meal you have found and prepared in the wild. But you must be careful. Do not put anything in your mouth that you cannot identify. Certain mushrooms are POISONOUS. Some leaves are HIGHLY TOXIC. A few varieties of nuts are INDIGESTIBLE. There are berries that are INEDIBLE. Mistaken identification could lead to DIZZINESS,

NAUSEA, VOMITING, or WORSE. Now, let's go find some supper!"

The Scouts wandered away from the campsite, unsure of where to begin.

"I feel ill," said Junebug.

"I don't dare eat any of this," Violet said, looking around her. She saw some berries that *might* be blackberries, but what if they weren't? And besides, there was a huge spiderweb on the bush, and the spider looked mean. She backed away.

"Are pinecones edible?" Petunia asked.

"I don't think so," said Hyacinth.

"Even if they were," said Junebug, "I'd never eat one. They house too many burrowing insects."

"This is going to be an awful dinner," Violet said.

"Don't worry," Cricket said. "We just have to wait until Miss Poppy is asleep, and then I'll get out my backpack. I think I brought enough cheese for everyone!"

At the thought of cheese for dinner,

the Scouts decided they were done foraging and headed back to camp. But just as they got to the clearing, they saw the squirrel rummaging through their backpacks. When he opened Cricket's bag, he squealed with delight, grabbed it, and rushed up the nearest tree.

"Hey!" Cricket shouted. But the squirrel was already up at the top of the tree. Cricket knew she would never catch him.

"My cheese!" she cried. "It's all gone!"

"NO!" shouted the rest of the Scouts.

"That's it," Tigerlily moaned. "We're going to starve!"

MOUSE SCOUT HANDBOOK

Building a Shelter

Camping outdoors is something every Mouse Scout should experience. Imagine falling asleep to the sound of the breeze blowing through leaves while in a soft moss bed in a shelter built with your own hands.

To build your shelter, you will need to gather some long sticks. It takes at least three sturdy sticks to build a frame for a tepee, five light to medium sticks for a tent, and several heavy sticks if you plan to build a cabin. Once you have your sticks, build the frame of your choice, referring to the diagrams on this page. Often, the quality of sticks you find will determine the style of shelter you can build.

Tent

Tepee

Cabin

When you have built your frame, gather pine boughs or leaves to create the walls. Grasses and vines work well for lashing the walls to the frame. You may even weave the leaves and boughs through the frame as if you are making a basket.

Pinecones can be used for roofing and siding. You can use them whole or broken apart like shingles.

Moss makes a soft and sweet-smelling bed. To be sure that it is dry, lay it in the sun while building your shelter.

CHAPTER 6

The Campfire

The hungry Scouts had little to show for their foraging. They each put what they had found in a pile. After Miss Poppy went through and eliminated the suspicious items, all that was left were three dried acorns, two clovers, and six pine needles.

Miss Poppy put her hands on her hips. "It's not much to work with," she said. "But we will do what we can."

She then supervised the Scouts while they built a camp-fire. "But *I* will light it," Miss Poppy said. "Acorn Scouts are too young to use matches."

Violet and Tigerlily made a grill by weaving some branches into a grid, and then soaked it in rainwater so the branches wouldn't burn.

Miss Poppy set the grill on four rocks placed by the fire so it would sit high above the flames.

Hyacinth and Petunia roasted the acorns on the grill, while Junebug and Cricket made a salad with the cloverleaf.

Miss Poppy showed the Scouts how to make pine needle tea by heating the pine needles and water in hollowed-out acorn shells. Finally their feast was done.

Junebug sniffed at the acorns suspiciously, then took a small nibble. "Yuck!" she said, spitting it out.

"It can't be *that* bad," Cricket said as she took a bite. She coughed. "On second thought, maybe it can."

Violet poured the tea into the cup from her acorn mess kit, but the cup was

cracked, and the hot water leaked
all over her lap. She thought about
the emergency sunflower seeds
and raisins she had packed. They
were supposed to be for emergen-
cies, and if this wasn't an emergency, she didn't know what was.
She put them out with the other food.

"Thanks, Violet," Petunia said, "but I
wish we had some cheese."

"I'm sorry," Cricket cried. "I tried to
catch that squirrel."

"It's not your fault, Cricket," Hyacinth
said. "But some cheese *would* be nice.
I'd love some Camembert or chèvre right
about now."

"Mmmm. Nothing is better than cheddar," said Tigerlily.

"But it wouldn't be a party without Havarti," said Violet.

"I can't tell a lie. I like Brie," Petunia said, joining in.

"It's pronounced *bree*," said Junebug.

"Oh!" Petunia said, blushing.

"Well, I think mozzarella is pretty swella," Miss Poppy said with a chortle.

The Scouts all turned to look at their

leader. Miss Poppy had never said anything funny in her whole life.

"I don't have any cheese," Miss Poppy
said with a sly grin, "but I *do* happen to
have some marshmallows!" She pulled a
bag of squashed marshmallows from her
backpack, and the Scouts scurried to find
sticks to toast them on.

"Ahem. Now, then," Miss Poppy said,
"it is time to sing. Let's start with the
Acorn Scout song!"

We are Acorns, tiny and small,
but we'll grow up to be mighty and tall.
We're quick with a plan,
and we help when we can.
We love our friends and are kind to all.

"Oh, that was so lovely," Miss Poppy said. "That song always brings a tear to my eye." Then she led them in singing the Mouse Scouts Friendship song.

Mouse Scouts, Mouse Scouts,
smart and clever.
Strong as Roquefort,
sharp as cheddar.
We work hard
to make the world better.
Mouse Scouts, Mouse Scouts,
friends forever!

"Well, Scouts, it's been a long day for this troop leader. We have to be up bright and early tomorrow, so I'm going to retire to my tent. You may all stay up a little longer and sing some more songs. I was young once. I know how it is."

Miss Poppy had a faraway look in her eyes for a moment, but then her spine stiffened, and her eyes got beady again.

"But two more songs *only*, and then it's time for bed. And that fire had better be put out properly or it's back to Buttercups for all of you!"

MOUSE SCOUT HANDBOOK

Campfire Cookery

Everything tastes better when you eat outdoors, and supper cooked over a campfire is doubly delicious. Whether you bring food from home or forage for your ingredients, you are sure to have a memorable meal. Remember that foraging for wild foods should only be done under the supervision of your troop leader.

Here are a few recipes to try the next time you go camping!

Campfire Grilled Cheese

(makes 6 sandwiches)

INGREDIENTS:

1 slice of bread, cut into 12 squares (for convenience, cut the bread into squares before your trip)

6 small pieces of cheese, whatever kind is available

DIRECTIONS:

1. Find a long stick—one that is shaped like a fork—to hold your sandwich.

2. Prepare the sandwich by placing a piece of cheese between two squares of bread.

– Bread
– Cheese
– Bread

3. Place your sandwich across the "tines" of your stick.

4. Hold the stick over the campfire close enough to toast the bread and melt the cheese, but not so close as to burn the bread. Be careful not to move the stick too much, or you may drop your sandwich!

Roasted Acorns

(1 acorn feeds one hungry mouse)

Acorns, the symbol of the Acorn Scouts, are plentiful in any forest where oak trees grow. Look for intact, unblemished acorns.

DIRECTIONS:

1. Crack your acorn to remove the hard shell. If you wish to use the shell as a bowl or cup, use a paper clip to scoop out the acorn pieces.

2. Place the acorn on a grill, or hold it on a stick over a flame. Turn the acorn often so that it is toasted but does not burn.

Pine Needle Tea

Pine needles are a good source of vitamins A and C. Not only is the tea delicious, it is also a good decongestant and, when cooled, can be used as an antiseptic wash. Any kind of pine needle will work, but white pine and balsam are especially delicious.

DIRECTIONS:

Take one pine needle and break it into very small pieces. Place the needle bits in your acorn cup and fill with water. Using a paper clip as a handle, hold your bowl over the fire to warm the water.

CHAPTER 7

The Ghost Story

The Scouts sat quietly in the glow of the campfire. Violet felt warmer and happier than she had all day. From the smiles on her fellow Scouts' faces, she was pretty sure that everyone was feeling the same way.

After a while, Petunia whispered, "Does anyone want to hear a scary story?"

"*Yes!*" said Tigerlily.

"Not particularly," said Junebug.

"As long as it isn't about cheese," said Cricket. "I'm so hungry, I can hardly think straight."

Violet's tail twitched. Cricket had had more marshmallows than anyone, but she wasn't going to say anything.

Petunia leaned toward the fire, and her face took on an eerie glow. She began the story in a low voice, just above a whisper.

"One summer night, many years ago, a troop of Mouse Scouts went camping. And this is a *true* story. I know it because my mother's neighbor had a friend when she was little whose cousin was a Mouse Scout, and *she* knew a mouse whose sister knew someone who was *on that camping trip*!"

"So what happened?" Hyacinth said through a yawn.

"Well!" said Petunia. "The Scouts had finished their supper and were sitting around the campfire singing songs and telling stories just like we're doing right now. Suddenly, out of nowhere, an owl swept down on the Scouts. And this wasn't just any owl either. It was a giant snowy ghost owl!"

"How could they be certain it was a ghost owl?" asked Junebug.

"I don't know, they just did," said Petunia. "And also, it didn't sound like a regular owl. It sounded all low and rumbly, like this . . ." Petunia took a deep breath and in the lowest, most rumbly voice she could manage said, "*Whooo* will be my supper? *Whooo* will be my supper?"

"Anyway, all of the Mouse Scouts were scared and ran into their tents . . . except for the smallest one. Her name was Peanut. When the Mouse Scouts got up the next morning, Peanut was gone, and *they never saw her again!*"

"That story's not even true," said Hyacinth.

"Precisely. There is no such thing as a giant snowy ghost owl," said Junebug. "Even if there were ghost owls, it would not be a snowy owl. They inhabit Arctic regions and are rarely seen at this latitude."

"But I told you, my mother's neighbor—" Petunia started.

Just then, the Scouts heard a low rumbling sound.

"The ghost owl!" they all screamed,
and dove for the nearest tent.

There wasn't much room in the tent, so
the Scouts huddled together, shivering in
fear.

Tigerlily looked around and counted five other mice. "Good, we're all here," she said.

There was another low rumble.

Violet whimpered. She took back all of the nice thoughts she had had while sitting at the campfire. She would *never* like camping!

There was another low rumble, followed by a . . . sniffle?

"Wait a minute, that doesn't sound like
an owl," Tigerlily said, sticking her head
out of the tent. As she looked around, there
came yet another rumble. The sound was
coming from the direction of Miss Poppy's
tent.

Tigerlily laughed.

"Some ghost owl—it's Miss Poppy.
She's snoring!"

MOUSE SCOUT HANDBOOK

Campfire Stories and Legends

No campfire is complete without a spooky story or two. Here are two classic Mouse Scout legends to get you started!

THE BEGGAR MOUSE

Cedar was a hard worker, even though there was never enough food to feed his wife and children. One fall day, Cedar went to the forest to gather nuts for the winter, but the squirrels and chipmunks had beat him to it. He managed to find only a dried-out acorn. He walked home wondering how he would tell his wife that they would have no food for their children that winter.

Cedar was so deep in thought that he almost didn't notice the poor old mouse sitting on the side of the trail. "Please, sir," the mouse said. "I am hungry. Can you help?" Cedar looked at the other mouse. He seemed very poor indeed, and Cedar felt pity for him. "I have very little," Cedar said, "but please come home and share supper with my family." The elderly mouse agreed. Cedar's wife set another place at the table and thinned out the parsley soup with water so there would be enough for everyone.

Even though it was a meager meal, it felt like a feast. The old mouse appeared to grow stronger with every bite. He entertained Cedar's family with story after story. Finally the hour grew late and the old mouse rose to leave.

"Must you go?" the children squeaked.

"We always have room for another," Cedar's wife added.

"No," said the elderly mouse, "but I thank you for your generosity." Then he turned to Cedar and said, "Your cupboards may be bare, but you are a wealthy mouse."

The next morning when Cedar went outside, he was amazed by what he saw. Alongside his door were a pile of fresh shiny acorns and another pile of walnuts. It was more than enough to keep his family well fed all winter. He felt wealthy indeed.

THE MOUSE OF THE MIST

One day, a young mouse named Lobelia was playing in a field. She was having so much fun that she didn't notice the fog rolling in until she was completely surrounded by mist. She had no idea which way was home. "Help!" she squeaked, though she didn't expect anyone to hear her. But someone did. Lobelia saw a shadow in the mist coming toward her. As the figure drew closer, she saw that it was a lady mouse dressed in old-fashioned clothing. "Your home is that way, my child," the mysterious mouse said, pointing into the mist. Lobelia hesitated, then skittered ahead. Soon she was out of the fog and could see her way home. She turned to say thank you, but the mouse had disappeared.

When she got home, she told her mother about the mouse who had helped her. Her mother gasped. "That was the Mouse of the Mist! Many years ago, her children were late coming home and she went out to look for them. A heavy fog rolled in, and neither she nor her children were ever seen again."

CHAPTER 8

Miss Poppy Is Missing

When Violet woke up the next morning, she felt surprisingly refreshed. She poked her head out of her tent and admired the sunshine sparkling through the trees.

The hike had been grueling, the meal was miserable, but the campfire was fun, and her moss bed was comfortable. Even Miss Poppy had been remarkably pleasant! Violet had to admit she was actually enjoying herself. Maybe there was something to the fresh wilderness air after all.

One by one the other Scouts emerged from their tents, rubbing their eyes.

"There was a root under my moss bed that kept poking me," said Junebug. "It was the root of all evil."

"I didn't sleep a wink last night," said Hyacinth.

"That's funny, because I thought I heard you snoring," said Petunia.

"I think that was Miss Poppy," giggled Violet.

Tigerlily was as full of energy as always. "Who wants to go for a swim before Miss Poppy gets up?"

Violet gave Tigerlily an exasperated look. "You know that would get us sent straight back to Buttercups, Tigerlily," she said. "And besides, the puddle has dried up."

It was true. Yesterday's puddle was now only a trace of mud.

"What are we going to do for water?" Cricket asked. "I need to wash the marshmallow off my face."

"We'll figure something out," said Petunia. "I'm sure Miss Poppy knows where to find water."

"Where is Miss Poppy, anyway? I thought she'd be up by now," said Cricket.

The Scouts looked at one another.

"She said we had to get up bright and early," said Petunia. "Do you think something might be wrong?"

Tigerlily tiptoed over to Miss Poppy's tent. She put her ear up to the leaf. When she didn't hear anything, she carefully pulled the leaf aside and poked her head in.

"She's not in there!" said Tigerlily. "She's *disappeared*!"

"The ghost owl!" said Cricket.

"That's the end of Miss Poppy," said Petunia.

"What are we going to do?" asked Hyacinth. "Does anyone remember which way we came from?"

"Sure. It was that way," said Tigerlily, pointing.

"I'm pretty sure it was that way," said Petunia.

"Did anyone think to bring a compass?" asked Junebug.

Tigerlily hung her head. It was the one thing she had forgotten to pack.

The Scouts all shook their heads.

"Uh-oh," said Violet.

"That means we're stuck here. Lost. All by ourselves," said Cricket. "We're going to starve!"

"Or be eaten by owls," said Petunia.

The Scouts sat in a circle wondering what to do. Suddenly Tigerlily jumped up.

"Wait a minute!" she said. "We're not doomed! What are we doing here? We are earning our 'Camp Out' badge. That means we have the skills to survive. We can do anything! We're MOUSE SCOUTS!  And we're going to find Miss Poppy."

MOUSE SCOUT HANDBOOK

How to Make a Compass

When you are in the wilderness, it is important to always have an idea of where you are in relation to the rest of the world. A compass is a handy tool for determining directions. If you do not have a compass, they are easy to make.

HERE'S WHAT YOU NEED:

A straightened-out staple

A small magnet (A small refrigerator magnet will fit in your backpack.)

A pencil eraser or a small piece of cork

A cup or bowl filled with water

DIRECTIONS:

1. First magnetize the staple by rubbing it along the side of the magnet in the same direction at least 40 times. You can test to see if the staple is magnetized by trying to pick up another staple with it.

2. Push the magnetized staple into the side of the eraser.

3. Carefully float the eraser in a cup of water so that the staple is lying flat. The magnetized staple will always point north!

CHAPTER 9

The Search

"Okay," said Tigerlily, rubbing her hands together. "First things first. Let's find some breakfast. We can't search on an empty stomach."

"But we don't have any food!" groaned Cricket.

"We'll have to try a little harder with our foraging," said Tigerlily.

Just then, they heard a loud cackling coming from the tree above them. It was the squirrel that had stolen Cricket's backpack! He held the pack up for them to see . . . and then dropped it!

"My backpack!" cried Cricket. "We won't starve after all!" But when she opened it, the pack was empty.

"Thanks for the cheese," the squirrel called. "It was delicious!"

Cricket looked so sad, even the squirrel felt sorry for her.

"Oh, don't cry. Have some nuts." With that, he tossed some beechnuts down to them. One of them bounced off Hyacinth's acorn cap.

Tigerlily gathered the nuts and started to crack them open with a rock. "Thanks, Squirrel!" Tigerlily said. "Breakfast is served, everyone. Bon appétit!"

The Scouts were hungrier than they had been the night before. "These aren't all that bad actually," said Junebug. It was the first time anyone had ever seen her eat without complaining.

When they finished, the Scouts tried to

come up with a plan to find Miss Poppy.

"Maybe we should each go off in a different direction," suggested Petunia. "One of us is bound to find her."

"It's too risky," said Hyacinth. "One of us could get lost. Or worse."

"Maybe the squirrel could help," Violet said. "He seemed friendly just now."

"Never trust a squirrel," said Cricket, holding up her empty backpack.

Tigerlily paced back and forth, scratching her head. They wouldn't be able to solve this problem with her emergency tool kit. They were going to have to rely on their wits.

Finally she had an idea.

"Let's walk single file in a circle around the campsite, making the circle a little bigger each time," Tigerlily said. "And don't get out of sight of the other Scouts. That squirrel may be annoying, but there are bigger animals around that are actually dangerous."

The Scouts walked in a circle and then a bigger one and a bigger one.

After they had made their sixth circle,

they heard a faint tweet. It stopped them
dead in their tracks.

"What was that?" whispered Cricket.

"Maybe it's the owl!" Petunia whispered back.

"Not logical. Owls are nocturnal,"
whispered Junebug.

"What if it's a raccoon?" squeaked Violet.

"Or a fox!" Hyacinth said.

"SHHHH!" said Tigerlily.

The sound seemed to be coming from a nearby bush. Tigerlily tiptoed carefully up to the bush, and the other Scouts followed behind her. She stopped and listened. There was another tweet, louder this time. Tigerlily peered into the bush, and there on the ground was Miss Poppy.

"Oh, Tigerlily! Girls!" Miss Poppy cried. "Am I happy to see you!"

MOUSE SCOUT HANDBOOK

What to Do if You Are Lost

Few things are more unsettling than finding yourself lost in the woods. The best thing is to prevent it from happening in the first place! Never venture into the woods on your own, and always stay on the trail with your troop.

Unfortunately, even the most careful Scout may someday get separated from her group.

If you become lost in the woods, do not panic. Your troop will soon discover that you are missing and begin searching for you. As you wait, follow these important steps.

1. Stop. Take a deep breath.

2. Stay calm and stay put. If you keep walking, you may end up walking in the wrong direction, making it more difficult for your fellow Scouts to find you.

3. Blow your emergency whistle every few minutes. Your troop will be able to hear you before they see you. The whistle will help them determine your location.

4. Take out your orange safety blanket. Not only will the blanket help to keep you warm, but the bright orange color will make you more readily visible.

5. Take stock of any food you have. Do not eat it all at once. Help may take a while to arrive, so be prepared to ration your food.

6. In the unlikely event that you are not found by the time it begins to get dark, build a shelter to sleep in. Try to keep a portion of your orange safety blanket visible at all times.

CHAPTER 10

Found

"Miss Poppy!" Tigerlily cried. "What happened?"

The Scouts crowded around. Miss Poppy was tangled up in vines and spiderwebs under the bush. Her arms and legs were scratched from brambles. Her hat was askew and her glasses were missing. Without them, she did not look like Miss Poppy at all! She looked scared and embarrassed.

"I woke up early and thought I would forage for our breakfast. I saw this blackberry bush, but I must have tripped on a spiderweb. The next thing I knew, I was on the ground. I tried to get up but got twisted in these vines.

Has anyone seen my glasses? I can't see a thing!"

Violet quickly found the glasses hanging from a branch of the blackberry bush. She handed them to Miss Poppy, then looked carefully at the vines around Miss Poppy's feet. Violet wasn't sure, but maybe . . . could it be . . . ? "Miss Poppy," Violet said, "is that poison ivy?"

"EEEEEEEK!" Miss Poppy squeaked. She tried to pull herself loose, but she was too entangled to break free.

Tigerlily took the twist tie from her pack
and used it to pull the poison ivy away
from Miss Poppy, being care-
ful not to touch the vines
herself. Violet cleared
the strands of the
spiderweb so no
one else would
trip on them.

Junebug gathered some jewel-weed. "It's a natural remedy for the effects of poison ivy," she said. She handed the leaves and stems to Miss Poppy so she could rub them on her arms, legs, and tail.

Finally Miss Poppy was free from the poison ivy and the spiderweb. But when she tried to stand up, she nearly fell. "Oh dear!" she cried. "I think I twisted my ankle when I tripped."

Hyacinth took off her neck scarf and wrapped it around Miss Poppy's ankle.

"That's better," Miss Poppy said, gingerly putting weight on her foot. "With a little rest, it will be as good as new!"

Then, using some twigs as crutches, Miss Poppy and the Scouts made their way back to the campsite.

Cricket and Petunia had gathered some blackberries and brought them back to the camp. As Miss Poppy and the Scouts dug in, they all agreed they had never tasted a better breakfast.

"Well, Scouts," Miss Poppy said, wiping blackberry juice from her whiskers, "you have more than earned your 'Camp Out' badges. I hope you have enjoyed yourselves and learned some valuable lessons."

"I know I did!" Tigerlily stated.

"And what is that, Tigerlily?" Miss Poppy asked.

Tigerlily looked at the other Scouts and they all said in unison, "NEVER GO INTO THE WILDERNESS ALONE!"

MOUSE SCOUT HANDBOOK

Wilderness First Aid

Hopefully you will never face a medical emergency in the wilderness, but it is wise to be prepared. With a good first-aid kit and a knowledge of a few natural remedies, it is possible to effectively treat the emergency until the patient can get medical care.

The following are some examples.

Emergency Bandage for Sprains:

Your neck scarf is not just a decorative accessory. It also works as a bandage for sprained ankles and wrists. You may also craft a sling from your neck scarf for an arm or shoulder injury.

How to Treat Poison Ivy:

Jewelweed, a common plant, is a natural remedy for the uncomfortable effects of poison ivy. Simply gather the plants and rub liquid from the stems and crushed leaves over the affected area.

Jewelweed

Make Your Own Bug Repellent:

Mosquitoes and ticks are not only annoying, they can carry diseases. Take preventive measures by making a homemade repellent. Mix two parts water with one part white vinegar. Add crushed leaves or a few drops of essential oils from mint, rosemary, or eucalyptus. Apply with a cotton swab. You might smell like a pickle, but you will not be bothered by mosquitoes and ticks.

Soothe Insect Bites:

If you do get bitten or stung by insects, make a tea of chamomile flowers and leaves. Apply to the affected area with a cotton swab.

Chamomile

The Badge Ceremony

The Scouts had an uneventful hike back to civilization. They each took turns helping Miss Poppy. When they reached the edge of the trail, Miss Poppy announced that a special badge ceremony would be held at the next Mouse Scout meeting.

On the day of the meeting, the Scouts all arrived on time, but Miss Poppy was nowhere to be seen.

"Not again!" Tigerlily groaned.

Then Violet pointed to the chalkboard. It read:

Mouse Scout Meeting Outside Today

The Scouts went outside to find Miss Poppy building a campfire.

"Scouts, as a special thank-you for helping me, we are going to celebrate your 'Camp Out' badges with campfire grilled cheese sandwiches!"

Violet nibbled the last crumb of her sandwich, then wiped her hands on the leaf she was using as a napkin. Her heart swelled as she looked around the fire at the happy, glowing faces of her fellow Scouts. Miss Poppy was right! *This is my happiest Mouse Scout moment so far,*

Violet thought as she scratched a little itch on her left hand. Then she noticed that her right hand was itchy, too. Violet took a good look at her napkin. "Oh no!" she cried. "Poison ivy!"

MOUSE SCOUT HANDBOOK

THE "CAMP OUT" BADGE

To earn this badge, you must complete the following requirements:

1. Pack a backpack for an overnight camping trip.

2. Complete a hike in the wilderness.

3. Set up a campsite.

4. Forage for food and prepare a meal.

5. Demonstrate basic knowledge of trailside first aid.

6. With the help of your leader, build a campfire.

7. Enjoy campfire merriment.

MOUSE SCOUT BADGES

Sow It and Grow It   Mouse Scout Heritage   Fun and Foraging   Make a Difference

Baking with Seeds   Take Flight   Dramatics   Signs of Fall

First Aid   Winter Safety   Predator Awareness   Camp Out

Flower Fashions   Weaving with Grass   The Night Sky   Friendship

THE ACORN SCOUT SONG

Melody by Frank Fighera

We are A - corns, ti - ny and small, but we'll grow up to be migh – ty and tall. We're quick with a plan, and we help when we can. We love our friends and are kind to all.

MOUSE SCOUT FRIENDSHIP SONG

Melody by Frank Fighera

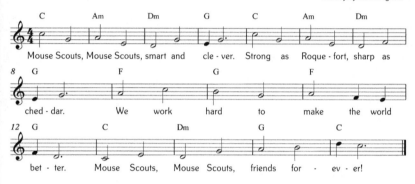

Mouse Scouts, Mouse Scouts, smart and cle - ver. Strong as Roque - fort, sharp as ched - dar. We work hard to make the world bet - ter. Mouse Scouts, Mouse Scouts, friends for - ev - er!

Sarah Dillard was briefly a Brownie and a Junior Scout. She fondly remembers making macaroni necklaces and, less fondly, one horrible camping trip when she had to eat the worst oatmeal ever. On the brighter side, Sarah studied art at Wheaton College and illustration at the Rhode Island School of Design. In addition to the Mouse Scouts series, she is the creator of picture books such as *Perfectly Arugula* and *Extraordinary Warren*. She lives in Waitsfield, Vermont, with her husband. Visit Sarah at sarahdillard.com.

The smallest Scouts with the biggest hearts!

Do you want to earn YOUR Mouse Scout badge?

Join Violet, Tigerlily, Hyacinth, Petunia,

Junebug, and Cricket on all of their adventures!

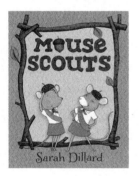 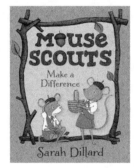 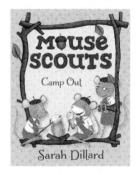